Polly Price

POLLY PRICE

Polly Price

D0002947

olly Price

Polly

Polly Price

P. Price

P.P.

Polly Price

Polly Price

Polly

P. Price

P.P.

Polly Price

Polly

Polly

Polly Price

Polly Price

Polly Price

Polly Prce

Polly Price

P.P

Polly Pria

P.P.

Polly Price

Chocolate mint wrapper from the aeroplane. I was going to save it, but I just couldn't

I bet I'll be seeing LOADS of kittens soon! CAN'T WAIT!!

luggage label

JET UK Boarding Pass

SECURITY No.	BOARDING AT	BOARDING GROUP
125		C

FROM	TO
LONDON/GAT	LAROCH/FR

FLIGHT	DATE
JUK4556	12/04/12

NAME
PRICE/HYPPOLITA-MISS

I **HAD** to buy these stickers as soon as I knew where I was going!

The **FATEFUL** toilet

POLLY PRICE'S TOTALLY SECRET DIARY: MUM IN LOVE
A RED FOX BOOK 978 1 849 41542 2

First published in Great Britain by Red Fox,
an imprint of Random House Children's Books
A Random House Group Company
This edition published 2012

1 3 5 7 9 10 8 6 4 2

Copyright © Dee Shulman, 2012

The right of Dee Shulman to be identified as the author
of this work has been asserted in accordance with the
Copyright, Designs and Patents Act 1988.

Red Fox Books are published by Random House Children's Books,
61–63 Uxbridge Road, London W5 5SA
www.**kids**at**randomhouse**.co.uk
www.**totallyrandombooks**.co.uk
www.**randomhouse**.co.uk

Addresses for companies within The Random House Group Limited
can be found at: www.randomhouse.co.uk/offices.htm

THE RANDOM HOUSE GROUP Limited Reg. No. 954009

A CIP catalogue record for this book is available from the British Library.

Printed and bound in China.

The Random House Group Limited supports the Forest Stewardship
Council® (FSC®), the leading international forest certification organization.
Our books carrying the FSC label are printed on FSC®-certified paper. FSC
is the only forest certification scheme endorsed by the leading environmental
organizations, including Greenpeace. Our paper procurement policy can be
found at www.**randomhouse**.co.uk/environment.

MIX
Paper from
responsible sources
FSC® C104723
www.fsc.org

DIAGRAM of aeroplane toilet

Aeroplane toilets just **AREN'T** big enough. Every time you try and rub out something or turn over a page you bang your elbows. → The seats are hard and narrow and not at **ALL** comfortable.

And it's very difficult to concentrate on writing when people

keep **BANGING** ⊷ ON THE DOOR.

They have been banging on the door so long now that I'm just too ~~embarassed~~ ~~imbarrassed~~ embarrassed to come out.

There's probably **35 REALLY ANGRY** ~~despirate~~ ~~desparate~~ **DESPERATE** people ~~cuing~~ queuing out there.

What will they do to me when they find out I've just been sitting here writing my diary?

Should I pretend to be really ill, and hobble out clutching my stomach like they do on TV?

AAGH!!

But they might think I've been shot, then go and get the captin and the plane's doctor and then they'd discover that there was no gun woŗund and they'd be even ANGRIER.

In fact they might put me in prison

for causing a TERRORIST ALKERT!!!

So I don't think I'll go out clutching my stomach.

I could just make a run for it ... but WHAT IF THEY CHASE ME?

Where could I go? I'M TRAPPED hundreds of feet in the air!

I'd have to run straight back to my seat, which just happens to be right next to MUM and ALMOND.

(What kind of a name is _Almond_? Surely it's a kind of nut not a kind of _annoying_ French person — though maybe his parents knew that he wouldn't grow up to be a normal human).

Hmmm - he's a bit nutty, we'd better call him Almond.

Oh well — the truth is — I can't sit on this toilet much longer. I'd better get it over with.

3

A FEW MINUTES LATER

+ Well, on the PLUS side — it wasn't 35 people waiting. It was 6.

− On the minus side — they took one look at my diary and pen and started shouting at me.

Especially the DRAGON WOMAN whose child had made a small puddle on her shoe.

But (on the plus side) — as I skidded back to my seat, with the 6 of them hissing behind me, it took one flick of an eyelash from **Mum** (who was probably a **GORGON** in another life) for them to give up the fight.

TOILET

As soon as she'd defeated my enemies Mum and Almond resumed their

STANDARD ACTIVITY

squishing themselves together
and ignoring everyone else (me).

ALMOND

is Mum's new
boyfriend. And
~~trajickly~~ tragically
I mean BOY-friend.
He SAYS he's **22**,
but I don't think
he looks old enough
to SHAVE, let alone
wind himself around
my (urgh) MUM!

Their faces have been virtually stuck together
for weeks! It is BEYOND disgusting.

AND... she's told him I'm her NIECE!
I'm not ~~aloud~~ allowed to call her Mum – I have to call her

Aunt Arabella!!!

How many mothers **DISOWN** their own daughters?
NOT many, I should think.

I did accidentally call her (Mum) yesterday.

She was **LIVID**

But Almond was charmed.

Ah, you zee – she lurves you zooooo mush that she calls you Mamma. It eez soo sweet!

Kiss Kiss Kiss

I think I'm suddenly HER NIECE because she's told him she's 27! And for some reason he believes her!

She's been telling me she's thirty-something for as long as I can remember – which means . . . by now she could be older than

40!!!!

A woman of her age should NOT be ~~aloud~~ ~~alloud~~ allowed to have a boyfriend.

Ooh, the seatbelt sign has come on. That means we must be nearly there!

6

We're on our way to FRANCE.

To a CHATTO. ← (I think that's the right spelling)

I don't know exactly what a chatto is — but I know that **chat** means **cat** in French so I'm guessing it's some sort of cat home —

Chat — to

cat — home

French and English are quite similar really. I think I could probably get the hang of French pretty quickly.

So if it's some kind of cat ~~sankchury~~ sanctuary there must be

KITTENS!

I LOVE animals. I'm really excited.

The chatto belongs to Almond's family. And he actually lives in it — so there must be bedrooms as well as cat baskets. This has to mean that although Almond himself is clinically insane (to be the boyfriend of my mother), his family are TRULY GOOD people to give over their whole home to cats and kittens.

Almond hasn't been back to France for a while because he's been working in England as an ~~acter~~ actor.

Which is how he met Mum...

LUVVEE!

DAHLING!!!!

...UNFORTUNATELY.

But all clouds have their silver linings.

I get to spend my Easter holiday with kittens and a load of truly good people!!! I can't wait!

We're LANDING! YAY!

MUCH LATER **10 pm**

French is a STUPID language! I <u>HATE</u> it!

And CERTAIN French people are CRUEL and MEAN because they laugh uncontrollably at innocent English GUESTS.

This is the <u>WORST</u> night of my entire <u>LIFE</u>!

And I'm in a freezing room, so will probably die of ~~hiper hypo hyperthermia~~ frostbite before morning.

WEDNESDAY 8.37am

Well, I did manage to ~~servive~~ survive
the night. I wore the entire
contents of my suitcase in bed.

hoodie

coat

jean jacket

shorts

PJs

7 pairs of socks

Not that **ANYONE** around here
would care if I did die.
They probably wouldn't even notice.
I could be lying frozen solid for 2 weeks before Mum spotted I
wasn't there to help her carry her
luggage home.

*Come along, Hyppolita,
I haven't got all day.*

And as for the rest of them... they would probably just LAUGH!
And personally I don't think it's **THAT** funny to ask
__IN A CHATTO__ where the **CATS** are.
But for some reason known only to The French, it turns out that
Chatto doesn't mean Cats' home.
It actually means ... **CASTLE!!??!!**

And this teeny mistake is apparently **HILARIOUS**.

HA! HA!

- HA!   HA!   HA!

9

HA! HA! HA! HA! HAHA!

And even Mum (who is meant to be my own flesh and blood) joined in with all the laughing last night.

As it happens I do not think the absence of cats is at all hilarious. I think it's extremely disappointing.

OK- I spose I shouldn't be one hundred per cent disappointed to find out that I am staying in an actual castle... But the trouble is The French don't really understand what a castle is meant to look like... →

No way is **THIS** a proper castle. It is IN FACT an **old ruin**...↓

It is **LITERALLY** falling down!

Here is a bit that fell off
my wall this morning
(OK – I slightly picked it off)

I am going to take loads of ~~dock~~
documentary pictures and stick them
in this book as evidence because I am pretty sure Mr Woodrowe
(the health and safety officer at school) would declare the
whole place

UNFIT for Human
Consumption

There are actually great big holes in the floor of the
room I'm staying in, which

FREEZING AIR
wafts through!

And half the banisters
are missing ⟶

PLUS the light switches are a
weird shape and they buzz scarily
when you try to switch them on.

This one is in my bedroom

11

I am now going to draw all the awful people in this chatto, because although I am freezing and starving I **WILL NOT** give them the satisfaction of going downstairs and asking for some breakfast.

Actually I have no idea what the French for breakfast is, and there is <u>**NO WAY**</u> I am going to guess.

HA! HA! HA! HA! HA! HA! HA! HA!

GLASSY EYE
(GLACIELLE)
Almond's mother
Laughs quite rudely.

TYRAN
Almond's dad.
Laughs **VERY** loud.

HORTENSE I think she's the housekeeper. I am not 100% sure she was laughing.

My fingers are blue and practically numb.
If I don't get out of here soon I will probably get gangrene.

A BIT LATER

Just when I thought I would have to give up and go downstairs, a visitor pushed open my door...

<u>DOG</u> →

(drawing dogs isn't my strong point so I thought I'd better label it)

He's very old and a little bit smelly but sooo lovely and warm. I have been defrosting against him. He doesn't seem to mind at all. Someone outside is being annoyingly distracting. He keeps calling something that sounds like Carlo.

11.30am

Well, Carlo - it turns out - is actually the correct name for my nice furry radiator.

And the person looking for him was... LUC~~X~~IEN

won't look in my direction

not at all smiling

chin in air

~~Lucyann~~ Lucien is Almond's younger brother.

Lucien probably would have been OK if he wasn't so cool (in a very BAD way).

Anyway, it turns out Lucien
got back from a tennis tornament
late last night.
With a friend. ⟶
Also cool-in-a-bad-way.
And sporty.
His name is unpronouncable
and unspellable. It sounds
like USE-TASS. So I think

I will call him ... | USELESS |

Actually he's not completely useless because
he speaks English. So does Lucien.
And they did say three very
PROMISING English words.

You want breakfast?*

*Breakfast is petit déjeuner in French — LUCKY I didn't try and guess
that one.

I'm taking this notebook down with me.

AT BREAKFAST

Lucien is telling Useless who everyone is — so I am pleased to say I have been able to add who's who next to the pictures I did earlier. Unfortunately writing labels only takes a certain amount of time. SO now I am having to ~~indure~~ ~~endure~~ suffer Mum and Almond's sickening displays of LOVE.

I am not alone in my disgust. Almond's mother looks like she's doing everything in her power to keep her ~~cwussonte~~ croissant down.

I've finally finished eating this  GIANT pan-o-shocolar

(I had to mention it because of all the chocolate smudges but I'm not 100% sure how it's spelled)

And I have just swung my leg round to make my getaway.
NOT QUICK ENOUGH.

Oh! The DAHRLING children! Of course POLLY will look after them while you go riding, Piranella! MY - er - NIECE just ADORES young children - DON'T YOU, POLLY?

Er... (NO)

And I am sure you two would LOVE to lend a hand, wouldn't you, boys?

Eh?

See you later, darlings! Come, Almond — You promised to show me the bluebells!

So Mum and Almond disappear off for a walk in the woods. (My mother walk? Yeah-right.)

←—Piranella and Gulle go off riding.

Glassy Eye goes to church... →

...and Tyran just disappears →

leaving the three of us to entertain Mimi and Jojo ALL MORNING.

Well – I say THE **THREE** OF US, but of course I actually mean THE **ONE** OF ME. As soon as everyone's gone, Lucien and Useless pick up a couple of rackets and balls and start playing tennis on the lawn.

So I am the one giving doggy rides to Jojo while he drips an endless stream of dribble down my neck...

...and doing rabbit races with Mimi **(NOT A COOL LOOK).**

To make matters worse, Mimi keeps insisting that we do our bunny jumps right next to the tennis game.

If Lucien and Useless weren't so obviously ~~conseeted~~ conceited I would have quite liked to watch them play tennis as – to be perfectly honest – they are quite good at it (especially Lucien).

But I am certainly not going to give them the satisfaction of having an audience.

LUCKILY Ortense - the person who seems to do all the work around here (apart from me) finally takes pity on me and calls us inside for some (really nice) hot chocolate.

(French translation: chocolat ~~shode~~ chaud)

TWEET TWEET TWEET TWEET

Just found out about the stupid silent H. If I can be bothered I will correct earlier versions.

~~Ortense~~ Hortense doesn't speak much English, but I understand this:

Come

I'm guessing a bird has flown into the house through one of the holes in the ceiling or wall. It must happen a lot, because Hortense doesn't seem very flustered. We quietly follow the sound. It's coming from a dowstairs room I've not noticed before.

Hortense ~~cortiously~~ cautiously opens the door . . .

In the ~~merky~~ murky gloom I finally make out Tyran (Almond & Lucien's dad — So that's where he went) putting little seeds into a bird cage. He turns round grumpily, but when he sees it's us he moves aside. We creep closer.

Inside the cage is a BEAUTIFUL canary!!!

Tyran puts his finger through a little door in the cage and the canary hops onto it! Then, very gently, he carries the little fluffy thing out of the cage and strokes its little head. He holds out the bird for me to stroke! It's soo tame!

Her name — eet ees ~~BEEJOO~~ BIJOU. Ziz is French for Jewel.

Then ~~Bejoo~~ Bijou does this little jump and is flying round the room, chirruping madly!

Hortense shuts the door really quickly so ~~Bijoo~~ Bijou can't escape and we all watch with COMPLETE joy!
The joy lasts about 20 seconds.

TYRAN! TYRAN! TYRAN!

The awful mother (Glassy Eye) barges in with the awful aunt (Piranha) and not very far behind are my mother and Almond.

Mum catches sight of little ~~Beejou~~ Bijou and actually screams!

Eek!!!

I am totally humiliated.

*!! *@*
* *!@ *

Then Glassy Eye starts this massive French **RANT** at Tyran - who growls and snarls back.

*!! *@*
* @ *

I have NO IDEA what they're saying to each other - but I can pretty well guess because Tyran really angrily puts out his finger, collects the canary, gently places her back in the cage, and shuts the little door.

The canary shouts tragically from inside.

Glassy Eye marches over, picks up a plastic cloth and throws it over the cage.

SILENCE.

Then she strides out of the room, followed by first Piranha (who gives us a full-on **piranha** stare), and then by my mum and Almond. To his credit, Almond does shake his head sadly and gives his dad a kind of ~~mornful~~ mournful smile. →

Tyran looks in disgust at the cloth and stomps out, leaving me and Hortense just standing there.

I am OUTRAGED!
Why was she being so mean

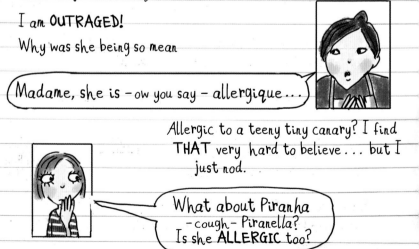

Madame, she is – ow you say – allergique...

Allergic to a teeny tiny canary? I find **THAT** very hard to believe... but I just nod.

What about Piranha – cough – Piranella? Is she **ALLERGIC** too?

I zink she just detests most leeving zings — particularly — bah — non I must not say...

Must not say what?

Non! Zat is — er — indiscreet... Come, will you 'elp me wiv ze déjeuner?

OK (whatever that is).

DÉJEUNER — it turns out = LUNCH.

There are many **many** good reasons for helping get lunch ready...

1) You get to eat lumps of the ~~gorjus gorgeus~~ gorgeous bread.

2) You get to eat bits of fruit that you are cutting up for the fruit salad.

3) You are not required to do bunny hops or doggy rides.

4) You get to give Carlo (the dog) bits of sosisson (sausage) whenever Hortense isn't looking.

5) You can ~~garantee garuantee~~ guarantee your mother and the boys won't turn up offering to help — so it is **VERY** peaceful.

It's a really sunny day so we take the food out onto the big wooden table in the garden. The adults drink **LOADS** of wine and start laughing quite a lot. Well, my mother does...

LATER

After lunch Carlo comes bounding up to Tyran, wagging his tail. Tyran laughs and winks at me.

> Ee wants 'is walk!

I look *longingly* at them setting off.
I would love to go. I've always wanted a dog. It looks like Lucien and Useless are planning to go. They put boots on.

Just as they're about to leave, Almond calls out something French to Lucien.

> Blah blah **Polly** blah blah

Something that has my name in...

Lucien turns to me, looking dubiously at my trainers.

> You want to come for ze walk?
> Do you 'ave shoes?

DUH!

Clearly these don't count.

He rummages around in a big box by the back door and retrieves an old pair of wellies.

I stick my feet in, but there's something inside one of them. I pull my foot out quickly. Lucien takes the boot from me, puts his hand in, and pulls out a tiny mouse!

EEEEKKK!

Blood curdling scream from... **Guess who?**

Lucien drops the mouse and it scampers into the sitting room.

EEEEKKK!! AHHHH!!

My mum screams more and runs out of the room.

I am **SOOOOOOO** embarrassed.

25

Let's go!

I say, putting the boot back on and making a dash for the back door. I have to get out before she does anything else ~~excrooshiating~~ awful.

The chatto is surrounded by grass and woods and hills. I don't know if this is all part of their garden (is it called a garden when it's this massive?) or whether they just live right next to the countryside.

After about 10 minutes of walking we move into the (very muddy) woods, which smell all sort of ferny.

Carlo is in heaven, sniffing trees, splashing in puddles and generally bounding madly around.

We follow him into a clearing which is COMPLETELY covered in bluebells.

It is totally → lovely!

Carlo spends ages bouncing around in the bluebells, while Useless and Lucien climb really difficult trees. I love climbing trees, but as I keep losing my boots just walking along the squelchy ground, I know there's no way I can climb in them. Anyway – they don't ask me if I want to.

So I hang around with Tyran, throwing sticks for Carlo. We actually have a really nice time. Apart from Hortense, he is definitely my favourite human here.

By the time we get back from the woods Hortense is giving Mimi and Jojo their supper.
I sit at the table with them feeding Jojo spoonfuls of jet-powered egg.

HA HA

And then I <u>help out</u>* with the bath time.

*This actually means getting squirted by a squeezy fish, making bubblebath beards and generally stopping Jojo from drowning when he decides he's a submarine.

I am **SOAKING** by the end of that adventure, so I have come back
to my room to change. But I have to admit that I think I'm
beginning to quite like being in a chatto in France!

> I genuinely felt that
> ~~BEFORE~~ supper...

LATER

I have been served up some pretty ~~atroshus~~ awful stuff at home...

slimy mushroom soup   lentil stews   alfalfa seeds   tofu...

...but waiting on my plate when I get downstairs is

rice (OK)

prawns in their bodies (not OK)

~~muscles~~ mussels (not OK)

s~~l~~callops (not OK)

octopus (not OK)

I look at it and panic. This is beyond **ANYTHING** I've ever had to
eat before.

Opposite me, Lucien starts dismembering his prawns
with his fingers and **sucking out their bodies!**

Eugh!

Then he spears the octopus
tentacles onto his fork and
chews them!

I am beginning to think I might be sick.

I take a piece of bread and nibble it.

I drink some water.

I shut my eyes, willing my plate to disappear.

I open my eyes ... It is still there. →

Lucien and Useless are discre~~t~~ely sniggering. →

HEE! HEE!

Everyone else is eating.

Even my mother. Who CLAIMS to be vegan.

I stare miserably at my plate, now wishing that I could

disappear.

> Preferably to my best friend Keira's house. We would be eating chicken nuggets or something else equally EDIBLE. And we would be having a conversation. In a language I understand.

Suddenly I am dragged back to the present by a nuzzling against my knee ... Carlo! He is sniffing my plate ~~appreshiatively~~ longingly.

Really ~~corshusly~~ carefully I sneak him a lump of octopus tentacle. He wolfs it down.

I give him some more. His tail thuds happily against my chair.

I eat a bit of the rice. I contemplate tearing the prawn apart and giving Carlo some of the pink body that's inside, but I can't bring myself to do it, and I daren't risk him choking on the shell.

But I do manage to scrape the snotty stuff out of the mussel shells and he licks it off my fingers...

CARLO I LOVE YOU!

Carlo's wonderfully helpful tongue

By the time Hortense comes to take my plate away, it looks quite respectable – just the prawns and mussel shells left!

But I am ~~exhorsted~~ exhausted by the stress of sitting there pretending that it's fun having nobody to talk to, while trying to look like I'm not feeding the dog my supper. So as soon as it's over I come up to my room. At least I am getting plenty of diary writing time.

THURSDAY APRIL 14TH

At lunch today I notice something . . .
Piranha NEVER smiles.
I suspect her mouth cannot turn that way up.

SHE HAS 3 BASIC EXPRESSIONS:

1) THE WINCE

The wince is on her face most of the time, especially when my mother says or does anything.

2) THE HUFF

Whenever one of her children or her husband head in her direction.

3) THE POISONOUS

She does her best to cover this one up.

But it flits regularly across her features, <u>especially</u> when she catches a glimpse of TYRAN   ALMOND   or   LUCIEN.

Tyran has just stood up
to take a tray of coffee
cups back into the house,
and Piranha's lips turn down
and her teeth glint as
Expression Number 3
takes hold.

I see Lucien stiffen – and I
know he has just witnessed
THE POISONOUS too.

But he doesn't say anything. He just gets up to
help his dad with the dishes. **Useless** has
followed him, and I am about to put my pen down and help
as well when

Jojo bounces onto my lap.

This is not a good feeling when you've
just drunk a pint of orange juice and eaten
a ton of French bread, cheese and sausage.
Luckily I've been wearing him out all
morning with more doggy rides so after about
30 seconds he puts his thumb in his mouth and falls asleep on me.

He is actually quite sweet when he's asleep!

32

Hortense – le babay.

ROUGH TRANSLATION – take the baby upstairs, change his nappy, and generally be the mother that I will never be.

Hortense is at that moment loading a tray with dirty dishes. She can't conceal her look of fury.

Piranha just carries on sipping her wine, eyebrows raised, waiting for Hortense to be her slave!
I stand up, careful not to wake Jojo, and sweep out.
My plan is to take Jojo off to his cot myself.

I have a vague idea where this might be because he was making so much noise refusing to go to sleep last night.

Unfortunately the chatto is big.
A vague idea is not very accurate.
And Jojo is **VERY** heavy.

So before long I have tried to push open about 17 doors with my elbow. 16 of them are locked and the 17th is a room full of junk with half the floor missing.

The situation is getting desperate... Jojo weighs a tonne.
I can't hold on much longer.

There is **NO WAY** I can skulk back downstairs **a TOTAL FAILURE.**
I need a plan - fast. And the only thing I can come up with is to
take Jojo to my own bedroom. Not the perfect solution, clearly -
but the **ONLY** one open to me. I turn round to
head back. A door ahead swings open. Lucien
and Useless emerge.

Useless **says**
something like → ... **voir**

Whatever

I'm still struggling towards
my room, when Lucien
doubles back and pushes
a nearby door open.

DA-DAAA!!! Jojo's cot

I can't begin to tell you
how relieved I am. And
obviously I can't begin to
tell Lucien.

Thanks

I mumble as coolly as I can.
He's gone.

As soon as I put Jojo down he starts to cry. So I pick him up again.
He puts his thumb back in his mouth and stops crying. I decide
to make sure he's really asleep - so I wander around the room,
with him snoring gently on my shoulder.

This is like an ~~anshent~~ ~~ancient~~
ancient nursery. There are
~~anshcient~~ toys everywhere and →
lovely pictures on the wall - but
the wallpaper has gone very
yellow, and there's the same
horrible smell as in my own room.

Right near the cot is a door that is a little bit open. I peer
through it. I DO NOT want to get caught nosing around. But
I AM ~~intreeged~~ ~~intreegued~~ intrigued.

It leads to a massive room. There's an enormous wooden wardrobe
in it with big mirrors on the doors.

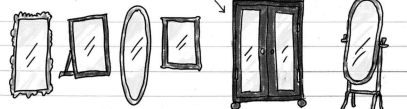

In fact I counted... 7 mirrors in here - all angled differently.
My mother would LOVE this room - she is no stranger to the mirror.

But if this was my mother's room there would be clothes and shoes and tights and hats and stuff all strewn about the floor.

This room is **EERILY** tidy.

Very near to me is a dressing table.

It has neatly arranged...

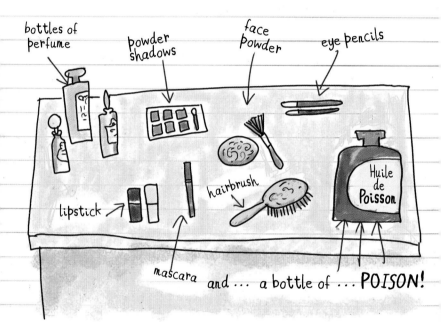

bottles of perfume

powder shadows

face powder

eye pencils

lipstick

hairbrush

Huile de Poisson

mascara and... a bottle of... POISON!

Why would anyone want a bottle of poison? Especially right next to the children's room? I hold tighter onto Jojo, and move away from the horrible stuff – towards this secret curtained bit...

I can hear a faint sound coming from behind the curtains...

I HAVE to take a peek...

I tiptoe forwards - every floorboard creaks, my heart is THUMPING so hard Jojo starts to wriggle - but I am so curious . . .

CREAK!

Uh-oh! Footsteps along the corridor outside!

I leap away, dash back through the door and manage to get to the cot at exactly the same moment as . . . Lucien arrives.

He looks at me suspiciously.

Why you still hold Jojo?

I look down at the baby - I'd nearly forgotten about him!

This is definitely the moment for an elaborate excuse.

Only I can't think of one.

brain
activity = 0

In fact my brain and mouth have decided to take this opportunity to completely shut down.

Not because I am trying to think in French.

The only French words I know are: BONJOUR and ~~CWUSSONT~~ CROISSANT.

(neither of which are very useful on this occasion).

The problem is MUCH more serious than that.

For some reason I can't seem to think in ENGLISH.

completely empty

I must be in shock.

Fortunately Jojo does this little snuffly whimper thing and I suddenly remember THE TRUTH

He – er – cries if I put him down.

Obviously I am not expecting sympathy from Lucien-le-Cool. That would be too much to ask. But I am not expecting him to LAUGH either. Sadly life is never quite what you expect . . .

HA HA!

Then he takes Jojo out of my arms and . . . WAAH!

HA! HA! Now who's laughing?

But Lucien cruelly ignores Jojo's misery . . . and puts him straight into his cot.

WAAH!

ME trying not to look smug

Lucien pats Jojo's back, strokes his head and **TOTALLY** ignores the crying. Then he pulls me out of the room.
We wait by the door, and about 30 seconds later Jojo goes completely silent.

He's probably suffocating!

strangulated squeak

I tiptoe back in...

Hmmm...

I am torn between **RELIEF** and **EXTREME ANNOYANCE**

that I've finally managed to put the weigh-a-tonne baby down

that L-L-C has succeeded yet again in making me look a *TOTAL* idiot

But my contemplations are suddenly interrupted...

Come on, Polly! Almond and your aunt are going to perform...

My AUNT? WHAT?!!!

39

As if life wasn't bad enough.

Throwing Lucien a look of total despair, I quickly head off in the opposite direction.

Escape is the **ONLY** way forward.
But forward, it turns out,
is not an option ...

– SUDDEN TUG –

↑
tennis player ~~mussles~~ muscles

AGGHH!
Really, Lucien,
I don't need to be there.
What's wrong with Useless?
Can't you drag him
along?

Usetass 'ee is
gone home ...
'Ee say goodbye
to you.

Lucien is looking at me like I have some kind of brain malfunction.

Typical of someone **useless** – NOT to be there the <u>one time</u> you actually need him.

I totally blame Useless now for the fact that I am being dragged towards my doom, with horrible images of what's ahead of me parading across my brain...

PLEASE! NOT a repeat performance of the Garlic Butter → TV Ad (this is how Mum and Almond met).

THE FRENCH LOVE... WINE, WOMEN AND... GARLIC BUTTER

or their ~~GARSTLY~~ GHASTLY version of Romeo and Juliet...

Romeo, Romeo! Wherefore art thou Romeo?

We've arrived at The Salon. ← living room
The WHOLE family (apart from the baby – how I envy him) is here.

Mum and Almond are not.

Is it possible my mother has suddenly realized that this is a **VERY BAD** idea?

I feel a little flutter of hope in my heart. It lasts for $2\frac{1}{2}$ seconds.

Quite a convincing death actually. I can't stop myself checking him for blood.

Then my mother walks in really slowly... and starts to ... _SING_.

That little flutter of hope has transformed into a sickening lump of horror...

Almond manages to keep up the corpse acting all the way through ...

At this moment death seems quite an attractive option.
Obviously not the Almond kind of death – in the middle of the living
room floor with your mother screeching horribly above you, and
various members of a mad French family watching ...if you can call
it WATCHING ...

↑ L.L.C.   ↑ PIRANHA   ↑ GLASSY EYE   ↑ TYRAN   ↑ GULLE   & MIMI ↑
sniggering   wincing   glaring   gaping   frowning   blinking

The only ones who seem to be enjoying it are –

HORTENSE   MUM and ... (I'm guessing here) ... ALMOND

I console myself with the knowledge that if my mother carries on
much longer we will be returning home to England very soon, and
won't EVER have to see these people again.

She finally sings her last note, does a stagey sob and falls dramatically across Almond. He tries not to scream in agony (he clearly hadn't been expecting this).

Lucien snorts and catches my eye. Why can't he just leave me alone? It is so mean to laugh at somebody else's afflixctions.

Mum and Almond are slowly rising to their feet. They bow.

BRAVO!

Polite applause from the audience (Hortense) gives me the perfect ~~oppertunity~~ opportunity to slip out.

I need to find somewhere to hide ... **FAST!**

Should be pretty easy in a chatto. But then I hear footsteps behind me – clearly other people are intent on escape before another song starts up.

I dart into the nearest room and shut the door. It's familiar...
Of course – there's the bird cage with the plastic sheet on it.
I tiptoe towards it, and lift the cloth...

Hello, Bijou!

Bijou is asleep on the floor of the cage. I put my finger in to stroke her. She stirs a bit. She is sooo sweet. She cocks her little head at me. Then she hops sleepily onto my finger.

I bet you'd like to have a little fly around, wouldn't you?

She flutters on my finger, and I am sure she understands!

Then I hear someone coming! And I realize I am about to get caught in Tyran's private study.

I look frantically around the room for
somewhere to hide.
The curtains are long and heavy.
I dash behind them.

The door creaks open.

I've been assuming it will be either
TYRAN $\longrightarrow$
(it **IS** his study after all)

or LUCIEN $\longrightarrow$
(come to gloat).

But it isn't Tyran or Lucien –
it's ... PIRANHA**!** $\longrightarrow$
What is **she** doing here?

She creeps in and carefully shuts the door behind her.

Then she tiptoes
towards the desk.
She's opening and
shutting drawers,
rifling through
the papers.

Chirrup
chirrup

Oh NO!!! I've left
Bijou uncovered!

PIRANHA glares at Bijou's cage, and
then looks around the room suspiciously.
I take a really deep breath and freeze.

BIG MISTAKE! The curtains are really dusty and smell AWFUL.

I can feel a cough coming...
HELP! I can't hold on much longer...
I'm CHOKING!

MAMAN! MAMAN! MAMAN!

Translation: Mum! Mum! Mum!

Mimi is shouting from somewhere
in the chatto.

Piranha looks
towards the door
furiously.

Then back to the
cage.

She strides over and
hisses at Bijou to shut up.

Sshh!

Bijou doesn't understand
and carries on chirping.

Then Piranha
starts shaking the
cage to try and
get Bijou to shut
up. This only makes
Bijou chirp more
frantically. She
must be so scared!

PHEW! What a narrow escape - for both of us.

Piranha returns to the drawers.

MAMAN! MAMAN!

Mimi is getting closer.

Piranha hisses, but carries on shuffling through the papers.

MAMAN!

Mimi must be almost outside the door. Piranha snarls, puts down the papers, and stomps out.

YAY! Mimi - I owe you one!

Freedom!

COUGH!

I practically fall out of the curtains, coughing my guts up.

COUGH!

I just want to get out of there the _fastest_ way _possible_. Which is through the window obviously. An instant ground-floor getaway... Or not. After 12 attempts I am forced to admit that the window is ~~COMPLETELY~~ COMPLETELY JAMMED SHUT.

Which leaves me only one option: THE DOOR.

I have no idea where Piranha is now.
Is it safe to leave?

What would **MAX VALE** do in these circumstances? ↑

CLEVER ~~AND~~ ~~REZORSEFULL~~ TEENAGE SPY
I find it quite helpful in life to turn to my fictional heroes for advice – bearing in mind that there's nobody factual around to give me any help in that department.

MAX VALE
Blasted

P.D. Ames

After a moment's deep thought I decide that Max Vale would probably crawl out on his hands and knees, thereby preventing detection from alien enemies. It is not easy to reach the door handle from down here – but yep – got it...

CREAK!

I've got the door open...

??!! I am facing a pair of knees...

... a waist ...

... (sigh) ... Lucien's face.

Er - bonjour, Polly.

smirk

PERFECT!

This SO wouldn't happen to Max Vale.

I pull myself to my feet with as much dignity as a person caught crawling on the floor can have. (None)

So? *

*ROUGH TRANSLATION
What are you doing creeping out of my dad's study.

Fair question.

What do I say???

Should I tell him about Piranha?

I think fast, and **TOTALLY** amaze myself by coming up with an answer.

I don't believe it! We have actually found something we agree on!

OK – does he mean: DO I **WANT** TO RIDE A HORSE?
Answer: YES

or: DO I KNOW **HOW** TO RIDE A HORSE?
Answer: NO

Well – how hard can it be? I say YES.

We meet my mother
(I mean **AUNT**) at the
back door.

Where's Almond?

Oh, he has to drive Maman to the marshay - er - market.

I only hope that one day, when I am ready to have children of my own, I have a child like Almond who PUTS A MOTHER FIRST.

(glint in my direction)

Come along then, children.

I breathe deeply and tag along behind, trying to think only of horses.

The stables - like the rest of the place - have definitely **SEEN BETTER DAYS**. There are bits of wood patching up the walls, and the roof looks - well - broken.

Inside it is quite dark but there's this lovely warm animally smell. I can hear snorty sounds and rustlings, and as my eyes adjust I can see that there are 4 horses, each with their own little room!

One comes towards us and pushes his nose over the door! Mum squeals and jumps backwards, but I am completely in heaven. I lean up and stroke his beautiful velvety nose.
He nuzzles my hand.

This is ~~Etwull~~ Etoile – it means – er – Star. You see here . . .

He's beautiful!

Actually **HE** is a **SHE**! We 'ave only one who is male – over here – Flambo . . .

Flambo is MUCH bigger than ~~Etwull~~ Etoile. Totally black. Totally shiny.

FLAMBO →

Wow!

Flambo, 'ee is my 'orse.

Then he shows me the other two horses –

MISTRAL (Tyran's horse) and **DIVA** (Almond's horse)

PIEBALD this means covered in patches of white and black – not a hairless pudding

MISTRAL – means Wind. This is because she runs like the wind!

the longest eyelashes EVER

nearly completely white

pink nose

Grey flecks in her mane and along her back. She is totally gorgeous!

So – we go riding?

Lucien looks at Mum's high heels and long dress. Mum, I realize, hasn't noticed. She has her eyes shut. Never a good sign. Lucien clears his throat and tries again.

So – we go riding?

Mum blinks and returns to Planet Chatto...
Lucien tries again...

Arabella - you like to ride?

She looks at him like he's the one who just landed on Planet Chatto.

I beg your pardon?

You come ride ze horse?

Ride the HORSE? Are you completely insane, Lucas? We don't ride horses! Limousines? Yes. Aeroplanes? Yes. The occasional train? Maybe. But horses?! Absolutely NO!

Could I look more humiliated?

Anyway, Linus - thank you so much for the - er - ACHOO! Come along, Polly - before the smell in this shed gets into our clothes and brings on one of my migraines.

She pulls me away. I turn round and catch sight of Lucien shaking his head at us, like we're both total losers, and I suddenly stop.

> Actually, Lucien, I'd like to ride...

I say in my loudest, bravest voice.

OK, that's how the words were meant to come out.
In actual fact they came out like this:

> Actually, Lucien, I'd like to ride...

My mother's face is thunderous.

> HIPPOLYTA! NOW!

But I stand firm.

> We won't be long— AUNTIE...

For the first time **EVER** my mother is *SPEECHLESS!*
She storms off, completely *LIVID.*

57

I turn back to Lucien. But instead of jumping up and down cheering, he is busy collecting loads of jangling things together. He hands me this incredibly heavy pile of leather stuff, with a black hat on top. I try not to stagger.

Right – you know 'ow to saddle a horse?

I blink back at him.

S-s-saddle a horse?

Should I pretend that I can?

I look down at this incomprehensible pile of leather and buckles and straps . . .

. . . And finally shake my head miserably.

To be honest (and I wouldn't even admit this to my best friend Keira), as I stand there I get that horrid prickly feeling behind my eyes and the trembly lip thing which means I'm about to start crying.

Sometimes you can stop yourself crying by telling yourself over and over again

I will not cry, I will not cry, I will not cry.

But I know this technique has failed when a big fat tear rolls down my cheek and plops onto the black hat I am staring down at.

I wipe it quickly away and do this kind of fake cough thing, to try and distract Lucien.

I think it may have worked, because he turns away and says in this really casual voice,

Er - Polly, I'm guessing zat maybe you 'ave never been on a horse?

I clear my throat. Can I trust my voice to come out normal? I stall for time, coughing and sniffing.

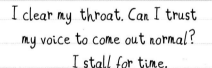

Well -er- actually... not exactly.

He does this sort of sigh, mutters Almond's name under his breath and takes the big pile out of my hands.

As if the day couldn't get worse, I find that I've started crying again, because in spite of everything I really had wanted to have a go.

I have to get out of here before he notices, so I head blindly for the door.

Hey-Polly, where are you going? I could do with zum 'elp 'ere.

I wipe my face and turn back round.

Lucien is leading Diva out of her stall.

But I don't know how—

You'll learn!

My fingers are all shaky, but he doesn't seem to notice, and after a while they start acting normally again.

I am totally glad I didn't pretend I knew how to saddle a horse.
Because **SADDLING** a horse is a bit of an understatement. It
actually means:

1) Brush down your horse's back
   really carefully.

2) Put a blanket-thing on and smooth
   it down, even when you can't
   see any wrinkles.

3) Put the saddle on.
   This weighs even more than a small child
   (I'm thinking of Jojo here).

4) Carefully fasten the strap
   underneath the horse's tummy.
   Make sure it's the right tightness.

5) Put on the bridle.
   This is quite difficult. Get the
   reins over her head and then
   start with the metal bit in the
   horse's mouth. Buckle the straps
   to the right tightness.

6) Pull down the stirrups –
   these are for your feet.

It is in fact quite (extremely) complicated.

Although Diva is way smaller than Flambo, that does **NOT** mean Diva is small. And now that I'm planning to get on her she seems to have grown about 100 feet.

I gaze up in **HORROR**.

Lucien just grins, cups his hands and gets me to step onto them. Somehow – and I still can't quite work out how – from there I manage to get whooshed up. Diva snorts and rebalances, which is a bit alarming, but Lucien strokes her neck and holds onto her reins, and she settles down.
WAYHAY! I'm actually sitting on a horse! And I feel like **King of the World!**

Lucien manages to jump the **500** miles onto the back of Flambo while still holding onto Diva's reins – which has to be an almost **IMPOSSIBLE** skill.

He shows me how to hold onto the reins and the front of the saddle, which makes me feel a bit safer, and how to grip with my knees. He tells me how to pull on the reins to slow down, and how to push gently with my heels to speed up.

COULD IT BE ANY EASIER?
HA HA! Only joking.
I am not stupid enough to
think I know **ANYTHING**
about riding a horse!
Which is just as well,
because as soon as we
start gently walking I
start wibbling around
like a BEAN BAG.

I realize that this is DEFIN~~X~~ITELY harder than it looks.
Lucien-Le-Cool does make it look INCREDIBLY easy, but he is much
nicer about my uselessness than I'd have expected.

He doesn't try racing on ahead, he stays right next to me, showing me
how to bob up and down slowly – which helps prevent the wibble
effect.

We walk our horses out onto a little path which leads to the
woods, and Lucien points out birds' nests and rabbit burrows.

I am **really** beginning to enjoy myself –
when suddenly a fox runs across my path.

Diva completely rears up
onto her hind legs,
neighing horribly.

AAGGHH!!

I grab onto her mane and hang on for dear life, while Lucien tries to grab Diva's reins. This startles her — and instead of settling right down she bolts away — REALLY fast.

I suddenly find myself GALLOPING through the woods at a TERRIFYING pace, clinging to her neck and trying to remember what horse language for STOP is. The thud of the hooves and the whooshing of the wind is sooo loud that I don't hear Lucien's frantic shouting behind me.

It isn't until the trees begin to clear that I become aware of him galloping up beside us, and though I am too terrified to turn my head towards him, I manage to tilt it a teeny bit. He is waving his arms, screaming —

He tries to bring his horse alongside mine. This is ~~vert~~ virtually impossible as we are travelling so fast. They nearly collide, which makes Diva even more scared, so Lucien moves Flambo a little further away.

DON'T LEAVE ME!

But he hasn't – he is now practically hanging off his horse and leaning across the wide gap to try and grab Diva's reins.

He swipes for them and… misses. Then his foot slips out of the stirrup and he starts **falling** off his horse!

NO!

Somehow I manage to twist my head and check on Lucien. **HE'S BACK ON!** I am SOOO relieved that something sort of clicks in my brain…

I know **I** can't let him risk that again. I **HAVE** to do this thing myself.

My hands are rigid around the horse's neck, but when I glance quickly down I can see a bit of the reins dangling not too far away…

Could I release my grip just a teeny bit and slide it along Diva's neck??

YES! GOT IT!

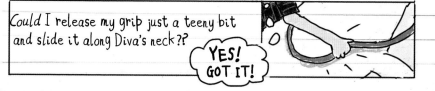

I now have to do the same on the other side, and I'm not so sure where the reins are there, and it's too scary to turn my head and look.

But I know I have to- so I try this very quick glance and catch sight of them - a little bit further away than the other side, but do-able.

This time, clutching really hard with my right hand, I move my left hand down across Diva's neck towards her head...

GOT IT!

I slide my hand with the reins in it back to the centre. The next bit is very difficult because it's almost impossible to pull really hard on the reins while lying sprawled across a horse's neck and clinging on like your LIFE depends on it (which - in fact - IT DOES.)

I said **almost** impossible, not **IMPOSSIBLE!**
Somehow I manage to stay pretty much flattened against her neck whilst shortening the reins bit by bit.

At the same time, next to me, Lucien is calling

Whoa! Whoa Diva! Whoa!

I join in too

Whoa! Diva! Whoa!

And gradually Diva calms down, and slows down to a trot, and then to a walk, and finally she stops.

We both sit there on our now still horses in silence for a moment trying to get our breathing back to normal. Lucien gets there quicker.

Well, you got onto galloping a little sooner zan I had planned!

I try to laugh, but my face has gone a bit stiff.

But – well done for staying on!

Yeah – **INSANE,** I know. But the truth is – although I've just been through the most **TERRIFYING** event of my whole life, it has also been the most *exciting!*

We walk our horses back towards the stable. There is a big water-trough outside it, and we wait while they both take long drinks. Then Lucien jumps off his horse and holds his hands up to help me off mine.

Naturally I jump athletically off Diva and land gracefully beside him.

IF ONLY...

If only this didn't have to be a **TRUE** diary. Then I wouldn't have to admit that my legs have decided to completely **STOP** working.

Actually, worse than that – they sort of lock in position and... **begin to shake!** Which means I am basically **STUCK** on the top of the horse!

Even my hands seem kind of **glued** to the reins. Is this ~~RIGERMORTUS~~ **RIGOR MORTIS**? I thought you only get that when you're **DEAD?**

And of course there's something <u>even worse</u> than being a shaking dead person stuck on a horse. And that's to be a shaking dead person stuck on a horse **IN FRONT** of **LUCIEN-LE-COOL.**

Er –
Polly?

PLUS – This horrible question is swirling round my head...
HOW DO YOU GET A SHAKING DEAD PERSON
<u>OFF</u> <u>A</u> <u>HORSE?</u>

Will they have to call the FIRE BRIGADE?

Will a French fireman dangle in from a crane and have to cut the reins free?
(I've seen rescue programmes on TV but normally the victims look **A BIT** more heroic than I do at this moment)

And will I spend the rest of my life in this position?

Lucien is trying not to look alarmed.

Perhaps you would like me to get some 'elp? Maybe your **aunt?**

NO!!

The thought of **my MOTHER** - or worse - **HIS WHOLE FAMILY** coming out and witnessing my shame seems to make my ~~simtons~~ symptoms **EVEN** worse!

I'll be all right in a minute!

OK.

I don't think this is the right word

Lucien nods and gets on with undressing Flambo. Whenever he's about to do something new, he strokes Flambo, and sort of warns him, in a lovely soft voice so that his horse never gets startled.

When the saddle and the bridle and the stirrups and everything are off, Lucien gets a towel and rubs his horse's back, and then gently brushes him all over.

He also does a kind of running commentary for me . . .

I do zis...

... to check he has ...

...no hurting place.

When Lucien has checked all Flambo's hooves, and led him through to the stable, he wanders over to me, and I realize my legs aren't shaking any more. And when he reaches his hand up for Diva's reins I also notice that my hands aren't stuck!

I CAN MOVE!

Lucien helps me down from Diva, like there'd never been a problem, and together we do all the unsaddling stuff, so that by the time we've fed the horses and set off back to the house, I have nearly forgotten the whole getting-stuck-on-a-horse thing.

OK this is a __SLIGHT__ exaggeration!

The sun is lower, but it is still quite warm when we reach the house. Hortense is setting the table outside for dinner. I say a little silent prayer for something **EDIBLE** tonight. I am **STARVING.**

Lucien and I go and wash our (FILTHY) hands and faces in the kitchen, then bring out the glasses and water.

Actually I nearly drop the jug I'm carrying when Hortense suddenly **BOINGGS** this massive gong. She could've warned me!

AGGHH!

Lucien **SNORTS** with laughter.

This is a bit disappointing after his extremely good behaviour all afternoon, but I suppose he can't stop being a boy.

Banging a massive gong, it turns out, is the way people in a French chatto tell everyone it's Supper Time.

The whole family (except me and Lucien) have changed their clothes.

PIRANHA selects a vampire outfit

Gulle drinks his in one noisy gulp. Naturally he gets awarded with- THE HUFF

But he totally ignores Piranha and holds out his glass for another. Hortense quickly refills his glass and ~~studiusly~~ studiously ignores Piranha.

I catch Hortense's eye. And the look she gives me fills me with foreboding.

Before the boys come back I know what they are going to say.

Bijou is dead.

Who on earth is Bijou?

My farzer's beautiful canary. He loves - loved this little bird.

I feel tears pricking my eyes. I'd only just met Bijou but I totally understood how sad Tyran must be feeling.

75

He doesn't come to eat with us, and his empty chair seems to send waves of sadness towards me.

I look at Glassy Eye. She doesn't look **IN THE LEAST** upset.

And **PIRANHA** looks positively **SMUG**.

How could they be so heartless?

Mum is just her usual sensitive self...

Are you telling me your father isn't coming to eat because his budgie has died? You cannot be **SERIOUS?!??**

I am soooo ashamed. I try to catch Lucien's eye to signal that I **DON'T** agree, but he gives me this really hostile look.

Then later, after the meal, I try to catch up with him but he turns round and moves away really quickly.

What is **WRONG** with him?
I am going to bed now and I'm feeling <u>quite</u> <u>miserable</u>.

NEXT MORNING (Friday)

I dreamed of horses last night and wake up all excited.

Then I remember Bijou and I'm really sad. And then I remember Lucien...
Why was he looking at me like he thinks I am to blame for everything?

GULP – that's it!

He **DOES** think I'm to blame... For Bijou's death!

He caught me creeping out of his dad's study yesterday!

He thinks I **MURDERED** Bijou! ———→

BANG!

Surely I wasn't the last person to see Bijou alive, was I? She was alive when I left the study. **WASN'T SHE?**

I try to think back. Something about yesterday is niggling. My heart is pounding, but I know I must not panic. **MAX VALE** is always saying that.

He says

> YOU NEED TO BE METHODICAL

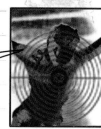

77

IMPORTANT ORDER OF EVENTS YESTERDAY

1) I go into the study.
   (Bijou is crashed out on the cage floor)

2) I wake her up and she hops onto my finger.

3) Piranha arrives and I hide.

4) Bijou starts singing and . . .

5) Piranha starts **SHAKING** the cage.
   Could this have killed Bijou?

6) No - because Bijou is still singing afterwards.

7) Piranha covers her with cloth.

8) Piranha leaves study.

9) I leave study.

Footprints

But then Lucien and I were away from the house for **HOURS.**
Anything could have happened in that time.

Maybe a murderer watching the chatto from a nearby tree crept
in? (None of the back doors are locked - **EVER!**)

Or maybe it was *An Inside Job?*

GLASSY EYE	and	PIRANHA

did not look AT ALL upset
at supper.

In fact quite the opposite.

Could one of them - or even **BOTH** of them - have murdered Bijou?

78

MURDERER'S MOTIVES

A murderer could have **LOTS** of motives.

Normally (in Max Vale books) someone in the family has done something terrible and the murderer is **SEEKING REVENGE**.

I wouldn't be surprised if there were lots of ~~Skelingtons~~ Skeletons in ~~Cupberds~~ Cupboards in this chatto (but I really hope there are none in my room).

GLASSY EYE'S MOTIVE:

1) She doesn't like birds (<u>CLAIMS</u> to be allergic)
2)

OK – that's all I can think of for her.

PIRANHA'S MOTIVE:

1) To keep Bijou quiet while she ...while she **DOES WHAT?**

WHAT was she doing ~~lerking~~ lurking in Tyran's study? She was definitely **UP TO NO GOOD**.

Maybe if I could work out what she was doing there, I could work out if she was the killer.

And <u>**CLEAR MY NAME.**</u>

So I definitely need to find out. The trouble is –
I don't think I am a **NATURAL SPY.**

I am sure that if **Max Vale** ←
was in a chatto he wouldn't keep
losing his way to the kitchen.
(Which I have done 3 times already)

He goes into all sorts of dark
and dangerous places without
getting even a bit scared. Plus
he quite often gets caught.
And ~~TORCHERED~~ **TORTURED.**
Which I **REALLY** don't want to get

So it's going to be very difficult to spy if I can't even remember
where I've been.

AGHHH!!! I've just remembered somewhere I've been AND
what's been niggling...

PIRANHA'S DRESSING-TABLE

This is totally **CONCLUSIVE!**
The murderer **HAS** to be Piranha!
And Bijou **MUST** have been poisoned.

blah
blah
POISSON

Actually now that I have worked out who my suspect is, I feel
SO much better. And more importantly it means I can <u>clear
my name.</u>

LATER (IN MY BEDROOM)

Well – **THE GOOD NEWS** is – my detective skills have definitely improved because I managed to find breakfast.

THE BAD NEWS is –

1) My legs and bum are in **AGONY** after the riding madness yesterday.

And . . . (MORE DEVASTATINGLY)

2) Lucien is **STILL** avoiding me.

WHAT SHOULD I DO?

A) Try and clear my name first?
   (by working out why and when Piranha killed Bijou)
      or
B) Tell Lucien who the True Suspect is?
   (Then he might be able to help me.)

B is definitely my favourite option for many important reasons:

   1) He's bound to have some **VITAL** information.

   2) It's much easier to detect in a French chatto IF YOU SPEAK FRENCH.

   3) I'd quite like to clear my name with him <u>sooner</u> rather than <u>later</u>.

   4) I'm slightly (very) scared to go snooping around the chatto on my own.

   5) I was just beginning to quite like having him as a friend (quite a lot actually).

81

A BIT LATER (AT THE TABLE IN THE GARDEN)

I have just spent the WHOLE morning trying to find Lucien.
He has **DISAPPEARED!**
I am totally scared that the **KILLER** has **STRUCK AGAIN!**
I have looked in every unlocked room in the chatto, and he's **NOWHERE.**
And as I am now officially investigating A MURDER (possibly 2) and
EVERYONE is a suspect (according to Max Vale), I can't think WHO to ask.

The only person I know couldn't have done it is Mum. I know this
because she has always told me that MURDER IS A MESSY
BUSINESS AND SHE WOULDN'T WANT ANYTHING TO DO WITH IT.
So I go and find her.

Almond on a big cool lawnmower

Mum, do you know where Lucien is?

Lucien? Who on earth is he?

Almond's younger BROTHER!

What — one of those children cluttering up the place?

Well, he's not exactly a child – he's **NEARLY 14!** It was Lucien who took us to the stables yesterday.

Sorry, Pettypie – children are simply all the same to me – and quite frankly the longer they are absent, the better. Make the most of it, I say. Oh, and darling, before you go – just cream my back, would you?

Obviously my mother isn't going to be much help.

I need to revise my view that **EVERYONE** is a suspect. It makes it too difficult to work anything out.

SUSPECTS

~~GLASSY EYE~~ ← I am pretty sure that Lucien's mother does not want him dead. She worships him.

~~TYRAN~~ ← So does his father.

~~ALMOND~~ ← I don't think Almond is the murderer either. He was out at the market during the ~~CRUSHAL~~ CRUCIAL time, and I can g^uarantee that when he is in the chatto my mother sticks to him like glue (in a totally sickening way).

But I can't **ask** Almond – I'm kind of avoiding him in case Lucien has told him I am the canary killer.

Hortense has just come out to lay the table. Of course – **HORTENSE**.
She loved Bijou and Lucien. She <u>has</u> to be a innocent.

Hortense – have you seen
Lucien anywhere?

Lucien? Non, Sherry, sorry.
Wiz 'is 'orse maybe?

Why hadn't I thought of that?
I sprint over to the stables.

ETOILE   **DIVA** and   **MISTRAL** are there.   **FLAMBO** isn't.

Phew! This has to be a **GOOD** sign. Surely Flambo wouldn't be missing
if Lucien had been struck down by **The Canary Killer.**

I squint towards the woods. No sign of him. He could be miles away.

I head back to the chatto, relieved.

But when Lucien doesn't come back for lunch, I start to get uneasy again.

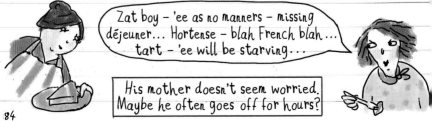

Zat boy – 'ee as no manners – missing
déjeuner... Hortense – blah French blah...
tart – 'ee will be starving...

His mother doesn't seem worried.
Maybe he often goes off for hours?

After lunch everyone goes out to some **Wine Festival.** Everyone **EXCEPT ME**, that is. I **HATE** wine.

They keep offering me watered down glasses of the stuff here.

But it tastes DISGUSTING!

So when Almond explains what happens at a Wine Festival (basically everyone goes round tasting wine) I decide it is **DEFINITELY** a pleasure I can live without.

Luckily Mimi and Jojo have refused to stay at the chatto, so I have **COMPLETE PEACE** ~~pirched~~ perched out in the garden writing my diary.

But the longer I write, the more worried I'm getting. Lucien has been gone for **HOURS.**

I pack up and head back to the stables. Still no sign of Lucien or Flambo. Diva nudges my hand when I come in to stroke her. As if she's trying to tell me something. Is she worried too?

I stroke her for a few minutes wondering what to do. Actually I'm not really wondering what to do. I'm wondering if I'm **BRAVE** enough to do it.

And for some **STUPID** reason I decide I am.

85

I go and collect Diva's blanket, saddle and stuff.

I half hope I can't remember how to saddle her, but for some reason I remember <u>everything</u>. I double check all the buckles and straps (as Lucien instructed yesterday) and . . . **UNBELIEVABLY,** Diva's ready to go.

BUT <u>HOW</u> DO I GET ON HER?

Stirrup - where my FOOT is meant to go!

I try to remember how Lucien did it yesterday. He put his left foot in the stirrup and swung himself up. **CAN I DO IT?** What if Diva bolts when I try?

I fasten her reins to the post, and go for it. All I can say is - Thank Goodness no one **Human** is around to witness this!

LUCIEN version

graceful and ~~adjited~~ agile

clumsy and embarrassing

POLLY version

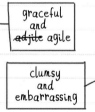

I finally make it on **ATTEMPT NUMBER 4**

My legs throb and my bum is *TORTURE* after all the bobbing up and down yesterday but at least I'm up here!

Right, Diva - let's go and find Lucien.

We trot around the grounds for a bit – no sign of them.
This can only mean ONE thing . . . GULP
I have to head for . . .

THE WOODS. →

BUM!
Even I know the woods are:
  1) dangerous
  2) dangerous
  3) dangerous

~~Espeshally~~ Especially when you are useless on a horse and don't
know how to find your way out.

But I can't let myself think these thoughts. I keep Diva's reins
tight, and try chatting to her in my least squeaky voice.

We wander around for **AGES.**

LUCIEN! LUCIEN!

I spot 5 rabbits, a million birds and
manage to get my arm caught twice
on some killer brambles.

blood →

It is beginning to feel like **YEARS** since I left my diary to come on
this stupid mission. And I have now given up any hope that Diva is in
charge and will make sure we get home. She is looking as lost as I am.

So I am slightly on the verge of **TOTAL DESPAIR**
  when I hear . . . a dog barking.

CARLO?!!

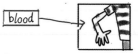

WOOF! WOOF! WOOF! WOOF!

Joyfully we follow the sound – though some instinct is telling me we
are moving deeper and deeper into the woods.

The path narrows right down but I manage to squeeze my way through — and there, just ahead of me, is...

CARLO!
What are you doing here?

But he runs ahead of me, turning back to check I'm following.

And just when I'm beginning to wonder what on earth I am doing — I suddenly see Flambo and —

LUCIEN!

Somehow I manage to get down off Diva.

Lucien! Can you hear me?

I put my ear to his chest. Phew there's a heartbeat. His eyes flicker.

Polly?

I am SOOOOO relieved! Then he groans and shuts his eyes.

WHAT SHOULD I DO?

He has a big cut just above his eye, and one of his legs is covered in blood. I'm pretty sure he needs to get to a hospital, but how do I get him there? If I go for help, will I ever find my way back here again?
He starts to try and get up, then gasps
Don't move!
I'm suddenly remembering all those TV hospital dramas -
You could have a broken spine!
A broken what?
he says, rubbing his head
OOOCH... OK, Polly - 'elp me up!
Realizing that my authority as a doctor is limited (ZERO), I do as he says.
He sways a bit, turns very white, but is definitely now ~~virtical~~ vertical.
OK - you 'ave to 'elp me onto Flambo.
WHAT?? You can't ride in your condition!

But I can't stop him. His bad leg is kind of useless, but his arms are strong, and between us, eventually we get him on his horse.

He is so slumpy I am really worried he'll fall off again.

I do my best to get onto Diva gracefully (3 attempts) and then walk her over to the slumpy Lucien. I take hold of Flambo's reins and we set off. Carlo bounds in front of us and I am **PRAYING** he is leading us back to the chatto.

After about 20 minutes of wishing I'd brought my phone with me, the wood start to thin out and I can suddenly see the house ahead. **YAY!!!!**

I give a triumphant look towards Lucien, but his eyes are shut. Carlo is barking like mad, and as if this is a signal everyone in the castle understands, Tyran and Glassy Eye and Hortense all come running out.

LUCIEN!

AH MON ~~DYER~~ DIEU!

French for Oh My God!

CHÉRI! ~~SHEREE!~~

I am pretty sure this is French for DARLING. They say it quite a lot

WOOF!

Tyran reaches up and grabs Lucien, then carries him towards the car.

Glassy Eye and Hortense follow quickly behind.

I just sit there for a few minutes in a complete daze.

WOOF! WOOF!

Then I twitch the reins of both horses and lead them back to the stables.

LATER

It takes ages . . .

desaddling . . .   brushing . . .   feeding and watering **1** horse

– let alone **2 !!!** (so I am NOT going to draw it twice!)

But **EVENTUALLY** they are both all snuggled up in their stables and I am back in my room.

Lucien and Tyran and Glassy Eye are still out (I'm guessing French Emergency Rooms are as slow as English ones).

I am Totally ~~Exorsted~~ Exhausted (but in a good way)
          Totally ~~Releaved~~ Relieved
    and Totally Starving.
                I look at my watch →

NO WONDER I'm hungry. I am going downstairs to find Hortense.

MUCH LATER

Hortense *looks* VERY grateful when she sees me.

She gives me some French loaves to cut up (I manage to sneak a couple of pieces into my mouth.)

And then she teaches me how to make a FRENCH DRESSING (This isn't something I am particularly grateful for — it tastes ~~GROSE~~ GROSS.) Not surprising considering the ~~ingrediants~~ ingredients

herbs   mustard   olive oil   dark red vinegar

I have just cut up a load of massive tomatoes when I hear the car pull up. They're BACK! Hortense and I rush out of the kitchen.

Lucien has DEFINITELY looked better

bandaged head

plaster on arm

bandaged leg

But he is upright (a good thing) and he manages a sort of smile.

Hortense bangs the gong and we all sit round the table for supper.

Almond and my mum come in giggling, showing no ~~compashion~~ compassion whatsoever.

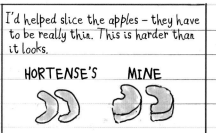

Piranha and Gulle come in arguing (has he found out about her ~~trechery~~ ~~tretchery~~ treachery?)

And Mimi and Jojo must already be in bed.

Lucien eats a bit of bread and pushes his plate away, but Glassy Eye makes him eat some steak. She is watching him like a mother hawk, which is kind of creepy but also kind of nice.

Definitely not something I have ever experienced. My mother usually has her own concerns.

Before we get onto the fruit tart Lucien goes off to bed.

I am slightly sad he doesn't get to eat any of the tart I helped with, but Hortense is saving him a slice.

I'd helped slice the apples – they have to be really thin. This is harder than it looks.

HORTENSE'S	MINE

Despite the fact that I have in fact saved their son's life, Tyran and Glassy Eye don't talk to me at all.

Nobody does.

To be honest, the only people really talking are my mother and Almond... if you can call it talking.

So it is another **AGONIZINGLY** long meal.

As soon as we've finished the tart, I race up to my room. Well – I say room but, as mentioned before, this is a very GENEROUS description. It is in fact quite hard to write a diary in these conditions.

The light bulb is very flickery and buzzy (which is quite distracting and also hard to see what colours I'm drawing with).

PLUS the damp smell is quite horrible (it actually seems to be getting worse). But a person who has managed to sustain life in her mother's wardrobe will NOT complain about a smelly, peely, dark, damp, freezing room.

I'll take a photo instead.

NEXT MORNING 9.05 am SATURDAY

I have just been woken up by someone knocking at my door...
AGGHH! What if it's the murderer? Should I open the door or hide?

LATER

IT WAS **LUCIEN!!!!** This is what happened:
         (I am going to write it like a play) ↓

THE ~~PORTENSHIOUS~~ AWKWARD VISIT

LUCIEN: (outside door) Polly?

POLLY: (thinking OMG OMG) Lucien?

LUCIEN: (politely) Can I come in?

POLLY: Er... (desperately tries to make **14 layers** of pyjamas, jumpers and coats look attractive) ... Yes.

   (*LUCIEN* enters, limping, eyes on the floor)

POLLY: How ARE you?

LUCIEN: Not so bad...

POLLY: How's your leg?

LUCIEN: (bravely) It isn't so bad – nussing broken!

POLLY: Er – **that's** good... So – er– how did it happen?

   (*LUCIEN* looks blank)

POLLY: (~~pashent~~ patiently) In the woods yesterday?

LUCIEN: Aw...it was all my fault. I tried to **make** Flambo jump **over** a big branch...'e refused... I fell.

POLLY: Oh.

The follows a LONG, **VERY** EMBAR**R**ASSING SILENCE.

   (**LUCIEN** stares down at his hands)

POLLY: Look, Lucien — I need to expl—

LUCIEN: Hortense, she want me to come . . .

POLLY: Hortense?

LUCIEN: To say — Zank you for . . .

POLLY: (goes **REALLY** red) Oh honestly Lucien – it was nothing.

> Yeah - right!

LUCIEN: I zink it was actually quite somezing . . . Anyway . . .
　　　　　　 (turns to go)

POLLY: (in panic) Lucien - don't -

　　(LUCIEN has reached the door. He stops.)

LUCIEN: What?

POLLY: Er . . . I need to talk to you about ~~Beejoo~~ Bijou . . .

　　(LUCIEN just stands there by door with his
　　　　　　　 back to ~~me~~ Polly)

POLLY: It wasn't ME who killed her –
　　　　 (For a moment it looks like **LUCIEN** is going to walk
　　　　　 out anyway. But then he turns)

LUCIEN: (with look of extreme disbelief) But I saw you
　　　　　　 leave the study . . .

POLLY: YES - but I'm sure she was alive when I left,
　　　　 and anyway - it wasn't ME that nearly
　　　　 SHOOK HER TO DEATH!

LUCIEN: What do you mean?

> OK, I've now had enough of being a ~~playwrite~~ playwright.

Worried that he will just walk out at any minute, I start to gabble. And in my determination to prove that I am innocent I even show him my workings out.

This is NOT a great idea – because he sees that I've written down HIS OWN MOTHER as one of the suspects.

BUT pretty soon (when I tell him about Piranha snooping around the study and the poison on her chest of drawers) he starts to look ~~thortful~~ thoughtful.

No-one can investigate on an empty stomach – so we hobble down for breakfast . . . One of us limping as the result of serious injury, the other as the result of bouncing around like a beanbag on the back of a horse.

LATER

OK - Lucien and I have come up with THE PLAN. We are claiming to be doing a PROJECT... about the chatto. This is pretty cunning because everyone keeps going on about the chatto and how to get it back to its FORMER GLORY - so it won't look in any way ~~suspicus~~ suspicious. Our plan has 3 SECTIONS:

A) <u>SPYING</u>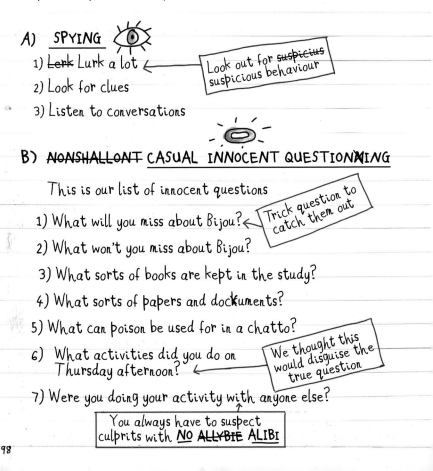
  1) ~~Lerk~~ Lurk a lot ← Look out for ~~suspicus~~ suspicious behaviour
  2) Look for clues
  3) Listen to conversations

B) ~~NONSHALLONT~~ <u>CASUAL INNOCENT QUESTIONNING</u>

  This is our list of innocent questions

  1) What will you miss about Bijou? ← Trick question to catch them out
  2) What won't you miss about Bijou?
  3) What sorts of books are kept in the study?
  4) What sorts of papers and dockuments?
  5) What can poison be used for in a chatto?
  6) What activities did you do on Thursday afternoon? ← We thought this would disguise the true question
  7) Were you doing your activity with anyone else?

  You always have to suspect culprits with <u>NO</u> ~~ALLYBIE~~ <u>ALIBI</u>

C) COLLECTING EVIDꟾENCE

1) Seize the poison from Piranha's room as | EXHIBIT 1 | → POIS

2) Try and find whatever docꟾument Piranha was looking for in the study.

> This should ~~connclusivley~~ conclusively prove her to be the guilty ~~perpytraitor~~ perpetrator

AFTER LUNCH

We have started filling in the answers to our inꟾocꟾent questions.

1) WHAT WILL YOU MISS ABOUT BIJOU?

TYRAN	Everything, especially her song.
GLASSYEꟾELLE	Nussing. She get on ze nerves.
HORTENSE	Aw la sweet thing. Such a shame!
PIRANꟾELLA	Birds are filthy vermin!
GULLE	What canary?
~~ALMOND~~ ARMAND	My farzer loved that bird.
~~MU~~ AUNT	Why would anyone miss a bird?

2) WHAT WON'T YOU MISS ABOUT BIJOU?

TYRAN	What?
GLACIELLE	What are you talking about?
HORTENSE	Aw – poor Bijou!
PIRANELLA	Polly – GO! Jojo – he's fallen over.
GULLE ↑	Eh?
ARMAND	Pardon?
MY AUNT	Oh do stop pestering us, children!

Unfortunately in the interest of *TACT* several names had to be modified

3) WHAT SORTS OF BOOKS ARE KEPT IN THE STUDY?

TYRAN	Many books — they have been in my family for years.
GLACIELLE	Too many books.
HORTENSE	So much dusting.
PIRANELLA	Polly! Jojo - he's hungry.
GULLE	I have no idea – this is Tyran's house.
~~AL~~ ARMAND	Ask my father.
MY AUNT	Don>t you have a horse to ride?

4) WHAT SORTS OF PAPERS AND DO~~X~~CUMENTS?

TYRAN	Many things – maps, photographs, letters, deeds, important family documents.
GLACIELLE	What did you say these questions are for?
HORTENSE	So much dusting.
PIRANELLA	(BASIC EXPRESSION NUMBER 3: Poisonous.)
GULLE	I have no idea – this is Tyran's house.
ARMAND	Ask my father.
MY AUNT	Isn't there a dog to walk?

suspi~~x~~cious

5) WHAT CAN POISON BE USED FOR IN A CHATTO?

TYRAN	Mice, rats . . .
GLACIELLE	Perhaps Hortense needs some 'elp in the kitchen?
HORTENSE	I don't have time for all zees questions, Chéris.
PIRANELLA	(BASIC EXPRESSION NO 3: Poisonous)
GULLE	I have no idea – this is Tyran's house.
ARMAND	Ask my father.
~~MU~~ AUNT	You>re giving me a migraine.

6) WHAT ACTIVITIES DID YOU DO ON THURSDAY AFTERNOON?

TYRAN	I don't remember.
GLACIELLE	Er – didn't I go to the ~~marshay~~ marché with Armand?
HORTENSE	Here – wash this salad.
PIRANELLA	(BASIC EXPRESSION NO 3: Poisonous)
GULLE	I have no idea – maybe I was sleeping.
ARMAND	Aw, Kids! Please drop it!
MY AUNT	I am not saying it again. Go and irritate someone else!

French for market

7) WERE YOU DOING YOUR ACTIVITY WITH ANYONE ELSE?

TYRAN	How would I know?
GLACIELLA	Tsk, I've just said! Now – AWAY!
HORTENSE	Here – carrots ... Peel.
PIRANELLA	(BASIC EXPRESSION Number 3: Poisonous)
GULLE	I doubt it.
ARMAND	(Dangerous expression)
MY AUNT	(Door slam)

Hmmm. That went well.

BACK IN MY ROOM

But Polly – we have got some useful information.

What?

My farzer's study does contain important family documents. Perhaps even his .... 'ow you say – **testament?**

Blank expression

Testament?

101

And maybe she would even...**KILL** to get what she wants?

We sit there in silence, realizing how scary the situation has become.

There's only one thing for it. We HAVE to find the documents before she does!

OK.

No time like the present.

We creep downstairs. Checking that the coast is clear, we tiptoe towards the study, and ~~vert~~ virtually crash into...

PIRANHA!

She looks a bit flustered and stalks off in the opposite direction.

Who clearly has the same idea.

The study door is shut.

Tyran spends the **WHOLE** morning in there.

Then after lunch we are told to get ready for **A HUNTING HORN CONCERT** at their cousin's chatto.

I am getting the impression this is **not** something to look forward to...

105

107

THE BAD NEWS When we get back everyone is milling around so we don't get a single chance to go back into the study.

THE GOOD NEWS Neither does Piranha.

SUNDAY APRIL 17th

YAY! Another sunny day. I am heading down to breakfast and ~~pracitcaly~~ practically collide with Mimi and Jojo.

They are running round manically and yelling –

PACK PACK PACK PACK

Does this mean they are LEAVING?
Which means **PIRANHA** is leaving.
Which means **THE END OF OUR INVESTIGATION!**

No more lurking and questioning and worrying about poison or the next murder victim!

I bounce into the kitchen. The table is covered in ... EGGS!!!

whatever that means

JOYERZ PACKS! Hurry into ze garden before zay all go!

Well, they must be in a major hurry!

I trot out into the garden.

POLLY!

Mimi and Jojo are out there now, shouting excitedly...

PACK!

When we've gathered all the eggs we can find, we head back into the kitchen. Most of the adults are finishing breakfast. They are all dressed up, even Hortense.

Egg rolling when we return. Are you ready, Lucien?

Ready for what?

Lucien starts talking to his father in French and I have NO idea what they're saying, but pretty soon his parents, Hortense, Piranha, Gulle, Mimi and Jojo all set off.

Lucien doesn't.

Where are they off to?

Of course - ze church. Eet is Easter!

You're not going?

My injuries! I do not wish to talk to all ze people in ze church about them...

Good point.

You know what this means, don't you?

He looks at me and smiles.
We set off towards the study.

Phaw! We should try and get a window open.

Eett smells really bad!

I think it's the curtains.

Lucien goes over to the heavy curtains and opens them. The window won't budge.

Oof!

But at least we can see what we're doing now.

OK – you check ze desk, I will searching these drawers.

photo of the study taken with my phone

I have **NO** idea what I'm looking for, but hope that I'll recognize something that looks like an important document when I see it. The desk seems to be COVERED in old photos. I stop rifling to study them.

We then spend the next half-hour going through all the pictures, Lucien explaining who everyone is, and where the photo was taken. We COMPLETELY forget we're supposed to be INVESTIGATING A CRIME SCENE and SEARCHING FOR EVIDENCE. It is not until the door suddenly swings open that we remember.

We sit there thinking.

Then I remember the other piece of evidence we're after –

THE POISON!

We've got to get hold of that too!

We creep back into the house. The coast seems clear, so we start up the stairs . . .

POLLY! LUCIEN!!!

Zey 'ave returned.

We stomp back down and join the whole family in the garden. Mimi and Jojo are REALLY excited.

FRENCH BABBLE BLAH! BLAH! BLAH!

What is going on?

It is Easter! We have to play ze games.

OK - I have to say one thing for the French - they definitely know how to celebrate! We've spent the WHOLE day playing LOADS of fun games ... Like -

Throwing and catching raw eggs in the air

raw egg!

rolling eggs down slopes

That's lovely!

Painting designs on eggs

PLUS I am now completely full after a MASSIVE dinner.

green beans

Carrots

amazing cake

potatoes

roast lamb

After dinner Lucien and I came up with a SERIOUSLY GOOD idea.
We plan to go into The Study at the **DEAD OF NIGHT!**

We are setting our alarms for `03.00` am.
By that time everyone
should be asleep.

3.05 am
I know Max Vale wouldn't be **AT ALL** scared going down a
decrepit creaky staircase **IN THE DARK**, and I'm trying really
hard to be **FEARLESS**, but I have to admit – this is a **TINY**
bit creepy. We've arranged to meet by the Study Door.
What if he oversleeps? Or his alarm doesn't go off?
I think I'll bring my diary with me to write down any important
~~dayter~~ data or facts.

3.10 am
Where is Lucien?

3.15 am
I'm going in.

TUESDAY 19th APRIL
IN A FRENCH HOSPITAL

They've just told me the good news.
I am alive.
WHAT HAPPENED?

FRIDAY 22nd April
STILL HERE
My head hurts
My arm hurts.
My leg hurts.
My shoulder hurts. It's really hard to write
with your arm in a sling.
Where is everyone?
I am scared.

SUNDAY 24th April
New ward.
Some of the tubes are gone. I can sit up.
I think they've said I'm getting a visitor.

LATER
Mum was the visitor. She spent the whole time
SOBBING. Loudly. My headache's worse.

She didn't mention Lucien. I'm scared.

MONDAY 25th April

OMG! I can see Lucien coming down the corridor!!!
He's ALIVE!
He looks frightened.
Who's that behind him?

LATER

It was the FRENCH POLICE!
They have just spent about 2
hours forcing me to remember
moment by moment everything
that happened on that
FATEFUL night.

They were in plain clothes so I didn't realize at first

Although I am ~~exhorsted~~ exhausted from their visit, I
am going to write down what I told them. Which is
exactly what Max Vale would do – even if his wrist hurt
and he definitly didn't feel like it.

POLLY PRICE'S ~~OFFISHALL~~ OFFICIAL STATEMENT TO THE POLICE

IT WAS **VERY** DARK – JUST A TINY BIT OF LIGHT COMING
THROUGH THE WINDOW ACROSS FROM THE STAIRCASE. BUT IT
MADE THE INSIDE EVEN MORE ~~SHADOWBY~~ SHADOWY AND ~~CREAPY~~ CREEPY.

IT WAS ALSO **QUITE** FREEZING GOING DOWN THOSE STAIRS IN
~~BEAR~~ BARE FEET. AND THE FLOORBOARDS ARE VERY CREAKY.
AND WHEN YOU CAN'T SEE WHICH ARE THE BROKEN BITS OF
BANNISTER YOU FEEL QUITE SCARED.

BUT I TRIED TO THINK OF THE INTREPID MAX VALE
AND MANAGED TO GET TO THE BOTTOM. THEN I CREPT ALONG
THE CORRIDOR TO THE STUDY.

THERE WAS NO SIGN OF LUCIEN.
I REALLY DIDN'T WANT TO GO IN WITHOUT HIM.
I HUNG AROUND FOR A COUPLE OF MINUTES.
MAYBE I'D GOT IT WRONG?
MAYBE HE MEANT ME TO MEET IN THE STUDY?
MAYBE HE'D GONE IN ALREADY?

I CAREFULLY TURNED THE DOOR HANDLE.
THE DOOR CREAKED OPEN.

LUCIEN?

I COULDN'T SEE A THING! IT WAS PITCH BLACK.
AND THE SMELL WAS AWFUL! I HOVERED BY THE
DOOR HOPING... a) MY EYES WOULD ADJUST TO THE DARK
b) LUCIEN WOULD SHOW UP
BUT NEITHER HAPPENED...SO I FUMBALLED AROUND BY
THE DOOR FOR THE LIGHT SWITCH—

Both the policemen looked up when I said this, and started scribbling madly.

Go on.

Then I heard a kind of fizzing — and a MASSIVE BANG... and ...that's it. That's all I remember.

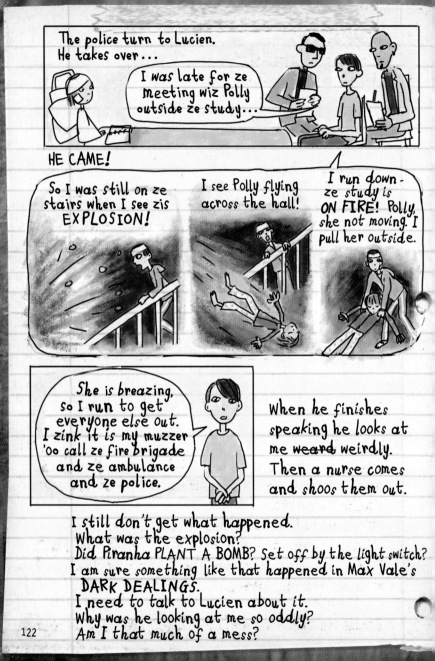

The police turn to Lucien. He takes over...

I was late for ze meeting wiz Polly outside ze study...

HE CAME!

So I was still on ze stairs when I see zis EXPLOSION!

I see Polly flying across the hall!

I run down-ze study is ON FIRE! Polly, she not moving. I pull her outside.

She is breazing, so I run to get everyone else out. I zink it is my muzzer 'oo call ze fire brigade and ze ambulance and ze police.

When he finishes speaking he looks at me ~~weard~~ weirdly. Then a nurse comes and shoos them out.

I still don't get what happened.
What was the explosion?
Did Piranha PLANT A BOMB? Set off by the light switch?
I am sure something like that happened in Max Vale's DARK DEALINGS.
I need to talk to Lucien about it.
Why was he looking at me so oddly?
Am I that much of a mess?

TUESDAY

They helped me out of bed today.
I saw myself in the mirror.

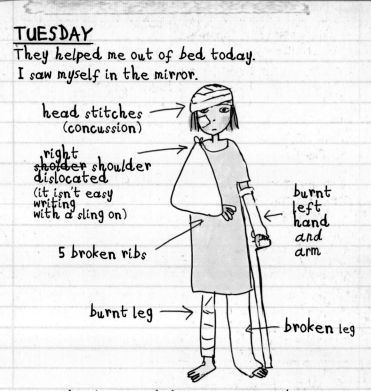

head stitches
(concussion)

right
shoulder shoulder
dislocated
(it isn't easy
writing
with a sling on)

5 broken ribs

burnt
left
hand
and
arm

burnt leg

broken leg

No wonder Lucien didn't want to look at me.

LATER

Almond came to see me. He told me the chatto
was so burnt that they had all moved into his
cousin's chatto.
It turns out that there was no bomb.
The fire was totally MY FAULT. Not Piranha's.
It was me switching on the light that caused a
massive gas explosion.

It was me that nearly killed EVERYONE in the chatto.

THURSDAY 28th APRIL

I saw Lucien coming along the corridor to visit so I pretended to be asleep. I can't face **ANYONE**.
Especially him.
He left some bluebells on my bed.

FRIDAY 29th APRIL

Lucien crept in today while I was having a dressing changed, so I didn't get a chance to pretend to be asleep. He brought a chocolate fish
but I am in too much despair to eat it.
I can't even look at it
(except to draw it).

dark chocolate

milk chocolate

white chocolate

I couldn't look at him either.
He sat there really awkwardly, trying to tell me bits of news.
He's tactfully trying to avoid mentioning the chatto.
He must hate me even more now than when he thought I killed ~~Beejoo~~ Bijou.

SATURDAY 30th APRIL

OH NO! I can see Lucien coming along the corridor again.
He's striding towards me, with a set look to his mouth. I think I am about to get my **BIG SHOWDOWN**.

LATER

This is how the showdown went . . .

I try to look at him.

125

For some reason I start to cry. I think it's because
I have been weakened by injury.

I sniff and smile. I suddenly feel a bit better. Quite a lot better actually.

NEXT DAY SUNDAY 1st MAY

Lucien is RUNNING up the corridor!

He looks ~~JOOBILLANT~~ EXTATIC OVER THE MOON.

LATER

I am almost too happy and excited and GOBSMACKED to write!
THIS IS WHY!

> I am going to write it like a play again,
> My hand was aching so much after doing
> all those drawings yesterday.

LUCIEN: (excitedly)   Polly – you never will believe this ...
(He swallows and shakes his head.)

POLLY: (with squeaky voice) Lucien, TELL me!!! WHAT????

LUCIEN: OK! You remember me telling you about

Ze Fongeaux Rubies ?

POLLY: (looking ~~mistyfied~~ mystified) The fairy tale?

LUCIEN: Well – SO I ZORT! But ze explosion caused ze wall
by ze fireplace to fall down, and – we found a
secret chamber ... And guess what was hidden inside?

POLLY: (hardly breathing) ... NO!!! I don't believe it!

128

LUCIEN: Completely correct! And we zink zay are worth a FORTUNE!

POLLY: Enough to get the chatto back to its FORMER GLORY?

LUCIEN: Quite possibly!

Exhibit A
The ACTUAL rubies.
Photo taken by Almond.

Unexpected HUG!

YAY!

POLLY: So – do you think Piranha knew about the secret chamber and was after the rubies?

LUCIEN: You are lucky you 'ave been in 'ospital. Zings 'ave not been good at 'ome since I mentioned that we knew she 'ad been in the study.

POLLY: You told them EVERYTHING?

LUCIEN: I HAD to. And also Piranella had to. Ze Police 'ave been VERY persistent. It turns out zat Piranha found an anskcient letter zat talked of a TREASURE MAP. She was convinced she'd find it in ze study.

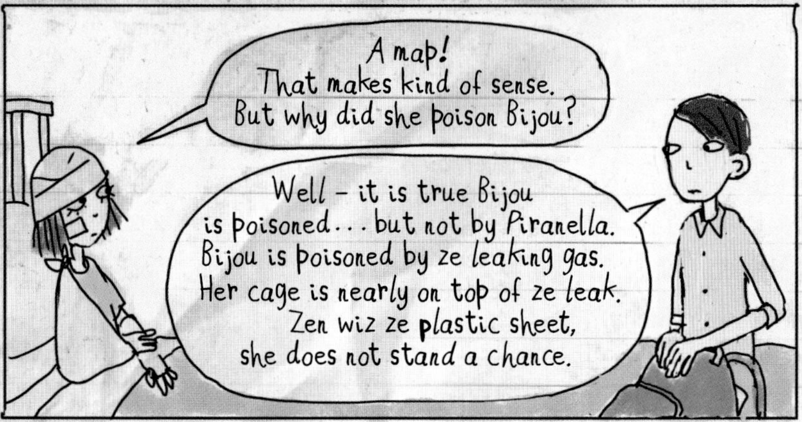
A map! That makes kind of sense. But why did she poison Bijou?
Well – it is true Bijou is poisoned . . . but not by Piranella. Bijou is poisoned by ze leaking gas. Her cage is nearly on top of ze leak. Zen wiz ze plastic sheet, she does not stand a chance.

But what about the bottle of poison in Piranha's room?
looking uncomfortable
Ah yes. The bottle.
Lucien rummages in his bag . . .

. . . and pulls out this photo.
Is this the bottle you saw?
HUILE de POISSON
Exhibit B
Poison on the chest of drawers

MONDAY 2nd May

They've taken off my sling and told me I can leave hospital! Mum and Almond are driving me straight to the airport. So I don't get to say goodbye to ~~Lucien~~ anyone. Which I am ~~very~~ a bit sad about.

So this is going to be my last diary entry in France. I am in the back of Tyran's Land Rover. It is not very easy to write because Almond is going round the bends so fast. It is also quite painful, because I keep bumping my injuries. But he and Mum are too engrossed in their conversation to worry about the invalid on the back seat. I bet Keira's mother would be a bit more attentive.

Why are we slowing down?

OMG What are we doing HERE???

The chatto – with EVERYONE outside!

Lucien told me this means WELCOME

BIENVENUE POLLY!

My hospital wristband.

PRICE Hyppolita 18/04/12

One of the bluebells Lucien brought me in the hospital

Gulle and Jojo

Tyran

Mimi

Mum

Piranha

Hortense

château

Lucien wrote this.
It turns out that I've been spelling Chatto wrong through the **WHOLE** diary.
There is **NO WAY** I am going to go back and change it now.

My champagne glass with Carlo pretending to be tired.
He **GENUINELY** *sleeps* with one eye open!

I think this is one of my best ever pics of Lucien

Polly Price

<u>P. Price</u>

<u>Polly Price</u>

Polly Price

Polly Price

Polly

Polly Price

Polly Price

P. Price

P.P.

Polly Price

Polly Price

P.P.

Polly Price

P. Price

Polly

Polly Price

Polly Price

Polly Price

Polly Price

P.P.

Polly Price